The Tiny Boy

AND OTHER TALES FROM INDONESIA

The Tiny Boy

and Other Tales from Indonesia

RETOLD BY

Murti Bunanta

ILLUSTRATED BY

Hardiyono

GROUNDWOOD BOOKS

HOUSE OF ANANSI PRESS

TORONTO   BERKELEY

Groundwood Books/House of Anansi Press
110 Spadina Avenue, Suite 801, Toronto, Ontario M5V 2K4
or c/o Publishers Group West
1700 Fourth Street, Berkeley, CA 94710

We acknowledge for their financial support of our publishing
program the Government of Canada through the Canada
Book Fund (CBF).

Library and Archives Canada Cataloguing in Publication
The tiny boy and other tales from Indonesia / retold by
Murti Bunanta ; illustrated by Hardiyono.
ISBN 978-1-55498-193-9
1. Tales — Indonesia — Juvenile literature. I. Bunanta,
Murti II. Hardiyono
GR320.T56 2013   j398.2'09598   C2013-900370-3

Design by Michael Solomon
Printed and bound in China

For children who love stories, and for those who bring them healing and nurturing stories.

CONTENTS

FOREWORD

The International Board on Books for Young People (IBBY) was founded by Jella Lepman in 1953. One of her core beliefs was that children who had experienced the disasters of World War II could be healed by reading great children's books from around the world.

Today this belief takes many shapes in the seventy-seven countries in which IBBY has national sections, and it continues to be a central tenet of the organization — bringing children and books together. IBBY's work with children in the aftermath of civil conflict and natural disaster is called the IBBY Fund for Children in Crisis.

IBBY believes that children who are suffering from natural disaster, displacement and war desperately need books and stories as well as food, shelter, clothing and medicine. These are necessities and are not mutually exclusive. IBBY's work with children in crisis draws upon the deeply held conviction that books and stories can change lives.

IBBY also understands how important it is for children to have not only great books from around the world, but also great books of their own — books that tell their own stories, that reflect their lives and cultures and are written in their own mother-tongue languages.

Murti Bunanta, the author of this book and president of INABBY, the Indonesian National Section of IBBY, has been a pioneer, both as a teller of stories from Indonesia's own extraordinarily rich and diverse cultures, and as one of the most effective organizers of programs for children in crisis. Due to Indonesia's location at the very heart of the Pacific Rim of Fire, the country has suffered destructive earthquakes, tsunamis and volcanic eruptions. Because of its complex ethnic mix, there have been periods of civil conflict.

Following the terrible tsunami of 2004, IBBY was able to raise funds from Mr. Yamada of Japan for an extensive project in Aceh Province in Indonesia. Not only was the province almost entirely wiped out by the tsunami, but its people had been in conflict with the central Indonesian government for a number of years. Within weeks, Murti had created motorcycle libraries loaded with books. She had translated a number of Indonesian folktales into Acehnese, and she and a team of volunteers arrived in the devastated areas with books, readers, love and bibliotherapy for children who had lost everything — even, in a number of cases, their parents.

Since then, after earthquakes and other disasters, Murti Bunanta and INABBY have brought Indonesian children the benefits of books of their own, and books from around the world. The children have been read to, talked to and helped to explore their feelings of loss and grief and to begin to resume normal productive lives.

All the royalties from this book will go to INABBY to support this extraordinary work. While we hope that Indonesia will be spared the worst, we can be sure that INABBY will be there if needed.

Patsy Aldana
President, IBBY Foundation
IBBY Fund for Children in Crisis   www.ibby.org

INTRODUCTION

Indonesia has a population of 240 million and includes three hundred ethnic groups, each with its own culture, traditions, customs and language. So it has a very rich folklore. But collecting and writing down these folktales can be challenging, as there are more than eight hundred indigenous or regional languages and dialects spoken by these ethnic groups. Only by translating the stories into Indonesian, the national language, can a large number of people appreciate their beauty and richness.

Indonesian folktales have many themes. The most popular are often stories about ungrateful children, as Indonesians are taught to be grateful, obedient and to respect their parents. But I have also chosen to retell little-known tales — some humorous, some traditional and some familiar. "Ampak and the Cunning Civet Cat," for example, is strikingly similar to the European story, "Puss in Boots."

Folktales are not just stories of the past, and I have chosen tales that are particularly relevant today. Although the most common goal for women characters in folktales seems to be that of becoming rich and marrying the prince to raise one's social status, "Princess Kemang" tells the story of an independent princess. An unusual model of a strong woman character in folktales, this is one of the few stories in which a woman not only chooses for herself the traditional pursuits of a man, but also proposes marriage to the prince.

In "Senggutru," a village girl no bigger than a thumb is able to defeat a giant. This story teaches us to accept and understand the odd and the small. "Masarasenani and the Sun" addresses an environmental issue, warning us not to be greedy about using the earth's resources. "Hua Lo Puu" deals with children's rights and teaches parents not to neglect their children. And although every Indonesian culture has a story about rice, the country's staple food, "Princess Mandalika" tells about the origin of wormlike sea creatures that become a useful, protein-rich food when dried and cooked.

The tales in this book have been collected and retold from oral sources as well as from materials found in old collections written in Dutch and indigenous Indonesian languages. Some stories have been retold from written materials developed by the Department of Education and Culture Project. The stories were originally collected from informants through oral interviews, recorded and translated into Indonesian. Now I have translated them into English. In my retellings I have tried to keep the language simple and straightforward, and to keep the meaning and moral of the stories clear and understandable. I hope you enjoy them, and that they will introduce you to the richness of Indonesia.

Murti Bunanta
Jakarta, Indonesia

Princess Mandalika

Once upon a time, in the kingdom of Sekar Kuning, there lived a strong and courageous king. The king ruled his country justly and wisely, and the people were peaceful and prosperous.

The day they had all been waiting for came when the queen gave birth to a beautiful baby daughter. They named her Princess Mandalika. To celebrate the occasion, a big royal party was held for all the people for seven days and seven nights.

Years passed, and Princess Mandalika grew into a very beautiful young woman. She was not arrogant and had great concern for the people's welfare. In return, they loved her very much.

One day, the king fell ill and suddenly passed

away. The peaceful situation turned into one of disorder. The king's two senior assistants, called patih, proposed that Princess Mandalika succeed the king. All the people accepted the proposal, and so the princess became queen and ruled Sekar Kuning kingdom.

Meanwhile, to the west of Sekar Kuning, King Johor ruled the kingdom of Sawing. To the east of Sekar Kuning lay Lipur kingdom, which was ruled by King Bumbang.

One day King Johor assembled his people. He wanted to hear whether they had any complaints. At first, no one dared to speak up.

Finally, one person in the audience spoke. "I am sorry, Your Majesty. All of your people are prosperous and living peacefully. But there is one thing that we are worried about."

"What's that?" asked the king. "Just tell me, and I will listen."

"Well, Your Highness," added another person. "We do not see any sign that Your Highness is making plans to get married. It would not be good for a great king like you not to have a queen."

All the people nodded their heads in agreement.

"All right," replied the king. "What do you propose? Is there anyone suitable to be my queen?"

Another person from the audience responded, "Forgive me, Your Majesty. I have heard that there is a Princess Mandalika who rules the neighboring kingdom, Sekar Kuning. She has just been chosen to succeed her late father. The princess is very beautiful, clever and rules the people wisely. And, she is still single."

"So what should I do?" asked the king.

One of his patih quickly answered, "We will deliver your proposal. We will leave early tomorrow for Sekar Kuning."

His patih soon prepared troops to follow them the next day.

It was the same case in Lipur kingdom, situated on the east side of Princess Mandalika's kingdom. The people were anxious because King Bumbang had not yet married. They, too, assembled to discuss who would be the perfect queen for the king.

Finally, an agreement was made. They appealed to the king, asking him to propose to the beautiful, just and wise Princess Mandalika.

The two patih of Lipur kingdom prepared themselves with their troops, and early in the morning they set out for Sekar Kuning kingdom, where Princess Mandalika reigned.

After some time, the two groups of ambassadors arrived in Sekar Kuning. Representatives of Lipur kingdom came from the east, while the ambassadors of Sawing kingdom came from the west.

The representatives of King Bumbang arrived first. They delivered the king's proposal to Princess Mandalika's patih.

After reading King Bumbang's letter, the princess asked the two patih to deliver her answer to their king. The patih withdrew. In front of the palace gate, they met with the ambassadors of Sawing kingdom, who had come to deliver King Johor's intention.

Now it was the turn of King Johor's ambassadors to deliver their king's wish to make Princess Mandalika his queen. Again the princess instantly answered King Johor's letter, and the ambassadors of Sawing kingdom returned to their country.

Both kings received Princess Mandalika's answer with pounding hearts.

And what happened? The princess rejected their proposals of marriage. She thought that she was not old enough to marry, and she wanted to stay near her people.

The people of both kingdoms were very sad to see their kings' disappointment.

While the people of the two kingdoms thought about the best way to console their kings, Princess Mandalika was in great distress. If she accepted the proposal of King Bumbang, it would make King Johor angry. On the other hand, if she accepted King Johor's proposal, it would make King Bumbang angry.

Since she had now rejected both of them, both kings might get angry. She was concerned that her kingdom might be engaged in a war with the two neighboring kingdoms, and all the people would suffer.

That night the princess had a dream. She dreamt that her grandfather came to pay a visit. In her dream, he said, "Wars can be avoided if you are willing to sacrifice yourself." Then he explained what she should do.

Princess Mandalika soon asked her two patih to invite the two kings to come to Sekar Kuning. The first patih went east and the second headed west to deliver the invitation.

On the given day, the two kings arrived at Princess Mandalika's kingdom. They wondered why the princess had invited them. Nobody knew.

Princess Mandalika welcomed the kings and said, "Well, King Bumbang and King Johor, after reconsidering, I have decided to accept your proposals. I will surrender myself at the time I have decided. Please come again with your people on the tenth month. I want to make sure that all the people will be present."

So both kings returned to their respective kingdoms.

Days passed, month after month, and finally the tenth month came.

Both kings left their kingdoms accompanied by their people. In accordance with Princess Mandalika's request, they all headed for the beach. The princess would welcome them there.

All the people wondered what would happen. How could Princess Mandalika surrender herself to two kings?

When all the people from the three kingdoms arrived at the beach, thunder roared and a heavy rain fell. But the princess was nowhere to be seen.

The people waited, anxious to know what Princess Mandalika would do.

The following day, when the sun set, a glittering light was seen in the sky.

Soon Princess Mandalika appeared, standing on a stone. The princess shone, and she looked very beautiful. While the crowd admired her beauty, they heard her say, "I have come to surrender myself, not only to the two kings who proposed to me, but to all the people who are present here."

Suddenly, a very big wave came. It swallowed up Princess Mandalika. The princess disappeared, washed away by the wave.

When they realized what had happened, the two kings instructed everyone to look for the

princess. People flung themselves into the sea. But no one could find Princess Mandalika's body.

They only found small sea creatures like worms, grouped together and shining like a rainbow. They looked so beautiful, it was believed that Princess Mandalika had been incarnated in the sea creature.

Since that time, Princess Mandalika has been called Princess Mandalika Nyale. Nyale means "to shine." According to the local people, along Kuta Beach in Tanjung Aan, many wormlike creatures can be found in February and March. The sea creatures are also called nyale, and they live in groups as big as tennis balls. And when they are dried and cooked, they provide nourishing food for all the people.

Hua Lo Puu

A husband and his wife lived in a village with their baby. Every day, very early in the morning, the couple went to their farm far in the woods. The husband gathered the forest crops, while his wife cleared the grass and bushes that grew so rapidly.

Each time they went to their farm, they took the baby with them, because there was no one to look after him at home.

One day, as usual, before they began to work, the wife looked for a shady tree with a low branch. She made a sling from a cloth she had brought to put the baby in. She hung it on a branch and the baby slept soundly.

The sun became suffocatingly hot, but the baby's mother paid no attention. She kept working diligently even though she was sweating all over. She did not realize that noon had come. The baby was starting to whine. He was hungry.

When she heard the baby crying, she worked even faster. She wanted to finish her work before she helped the baby. She was so deeply occupied that she no longer heard her baby's cry among the twitters and shrieks of the birds in the woods.

In the meantime, the birds were drawn to the baby's cry. One at a time they descended from one branch to the next until they were close to the baby's sling, as if they wanted to know what kind of creature was hidden inside.

Finally, a bird summoned the courage to perch on the edge of the sling. All the other birds followed, whistling as they took turns coming closer to look at the crying baby. Seeing the helpless baby wrapped only in a piece of cloth, the birds felt compassion. They thought the baby must be cold.

One of the biggest birds began to drop some of his feathers into the sling. Soon all the other birds did the same.

In seconds, the baby was almost covered with beautiful feathers of all colors. He stopped crying. The softness of the feathers kept him comfortable and warm. He felt that somebody cared for him.

When the mother heard no more crying, she

thought the baby had fallen asleep. So she continued to work, intending to check on her baby when he awoke.

Suddenly, she was startled by the sound of a strange bird twittering among the usual bird voices. The sound seemed sorrowful and sad. *"Hua ... lo ... puu! Hua ... lo ... puu!"*

This long, sad voice moved her. When she heard it again, she realized that it came from the tree where she had hung the sling.

She stopped her work and hurried to her baby.

When she came to the sling, she found it empty. Then she saw on the tip of the tree a small bird with beautiful feathers flying from one branch to another. It sang very long and sorrowfully. *"Hua ... lo ... puu. Hua ... lo ... puu!* My dear mother ... don't look for your baby anymore. It's me ... "

The mother was shocked and saddened. She sobbed, calling, "Come back, my child! Come back, my dear! I want to cradle you. I will nurse you!"

But the little bird kept flying from one branch to another, singing, *"Hua ... lo ... puu! Hua ... lo ... puu!* Don't cry, my mother, dear! *Hua ... lo ... puu!"*

When her husband came back from gathering the forest crops, his wife told him what had happened. The sad couple kept trying to make their child become human again. But their efforts were all in vain. They were only comforted by the fact that their child was still alive as a tiny bird with beautiful feathers, who would always be near them.

Because the day was getting dark, the couple went home. They were followed by the small beautiful bird, singing, *"Hua ... lo ... puu! Hua... lo ... puu!"*

The people in the village were surprised to hear what had happened. After that, all the villagers paid more attention to their own children, especially the babies. And from that time on, no one teased, caught or sold the birds that lived in their village. They were especially kind to the little ones, because the birds had once taken care of a helpless baby who needed affection.

The Legend
of the Banyan Tree

Once upon a time, there was a brave king who reigned over one of the biggest kingdoms on the island of Java. He could defeat his enemies with swords and spears or with a mere dagger. It was said that he could catch more than fifty arrows with his bare hands. He had conquered many countries.

The king had a queen and several concubines. With the queen, he had a prince named Jamojaya, and with his most beautiful concubine, named Dewi Andana, he had a son named Raden Samijaya. The beauty of Dewi Andana exceeded the beauty of the queen and all the other concubines. She was also the one most deeply loved by the king. He often gave her jewelry and other expensive gifts.

The prince, Jamojaya, was loved and honored by all his people for his handsomeness, bravery and strength. Moreover, he was very kind to everyone.

Unfortunately, Dewi Andana hated Jamojaya. She was jealous because her son, Raden Samijaya, was not a prince. Dewi Andana was afraid that when the king died, Prince Jamojaya would succeed him, and she and her son might be thrown out of the palace.

So she wanted to find a way to get rid of Prince Jamojaya.

One day, when the king visited Dewi Andana, she pretended to look sad. When the king asked why she was sad, Dewi Andana said, "Forgive me, Your Highness. I have received so many beautiful and expensive gifts from you, but I still have one unfulfilled wish."

"Say what you want, Dewi Andana. Your wish shall be granted," replied the king.

"I want my son, Raden Samijaya, to become your heir," she said in a forceful tone.

The king was very surprised at her wish and, despite his promise, he refused to fulfill her desire. It was impossible for Raden Samijaya to replace his brother, Jamojaya, for Raden Samijaya was not a prince.

But Dewi Andana would not be silenced. "Your Highness, if Prince Jamojaya rules, all your concubines will be expelled, and you won't see me again. To avoid this, please tell Prince Jamojaya that someone is plotting to poison him, so he will leave the palace."

Constantly nagged by Dewi Andana, the king finally gave in. He called Prince Jamojaya and told him that the prince must leave the palace immediately.

"Father, let me stay," the prince begged. "I am not afraid of being killed if that is to be my destiny."

But the king stuck to his decision, and no one could change his mind.

Prince Jamojaya sought out his wife, Princess Kusumasari, and told her about the king's decision.

"Dewi Kusumasari, my wife, I have been asked to leave the palace. Although I have told the king that I am not afraid of being killed and want to stay, he has refused to allow me to do so. I have to depart very soon. Since I will have to travel a long distance, it would be better for you to stay in the palace."

But Dewi Kusumasari was determined to go with her husband.

While Prince Jamojaya was talking to Dewi Kusumasari, Dewi Andana crept into the prince's room. She was worried that the king would change his mind. She slipped poison into Jamojaya's drinking water, which he kept in a kendi, a clay pot near his bed. Then she hurried out of the room.

That night the prince felt thirsty, and he drank the poisoned water.

When Prince Jamojaya awoke the following day, he felt tired and had a headache, but he did not tell anyone about his condition. A few days later, he left the palace accompanied only by Dewi Kusumasari. No bodyguards attended them as they went.

Every day of the journey Prince Jamojaya grew weaker. Although he felt sick, he gallantly kept walking into the forest beside his wife.

Finally, the day came when he could no longer keep going, and he died.

Dewi Kusumasari was very sad. Kneeling beside her husband, she wept and prayed for help from the gods in heaven.

Hearing her lamentation and prayer, the God Kamajaya, the Protector of Marriage, was touched, and he descended from heaven. When Dewi Kusumasari noticed the God Kamajaya standing near Prince Jamojaya's body, she begged, "God Kamajaya, have mercy and bring my husband to life again!"

The God Kamajaya answered sadly, "I am sorry I cannot fulfill your wish, my child! Prince Jamojaya has drunk strongly poisoned water. No gods will be able to cure him. But to make him live forever on earth, I will change him into a strong and beautiful tree that will grow in this very place."

Suddenly, Prince Jamojaya's body stood upright with outstretched arms. His body was covered by rough skin, and from his arms sprang green leaves. His long black hair became tangled roots that touched the ground. His legs disappeared into the earth, becoming underground roots.

Dewi Kusumasari was not comforted by this strange tree.

"What is this lifeless tree for? This is not my husband."

Then the God Kamajaya said, "Dewi Kusumasari, my child, this tree is not lifeless. It will be called Beringin, the banyan tree, and it will live forever. People will consider this tree sacred and put offerings for the gods under its branches. Kings who are weary of fighting wars will rest under the banyan tree and listen to the rustling of its leaves. Children will play in it, and young people will talk with their friends in its shade. But if any should dare cut down this tree, his descendants shall be cursed. They will sicken or suffer accidents before they grow up."

Then the God Kamajaya flew back to heaven, leaving Dewi Kusumasari to her mourning.

In her sorrow, Dewi Kusumasari approached the banyan tree, which was the incarnation of her husband, and hugged its trunk. Then she laid her head against it and went to sleep forever. Her soul was welcomed into heaven, while her body turned into a spring of very clear water.

Meanwhile, in the kingdom, the people were anxious about the loss of the prince whom they loved so much. When the king announced that Raden Samijaya would succeed to the throne when he died, the people learned that Prince Jamojaya had been forced into exile. They wanted Prince Jamojaya back in the palace, and they grew so angry that riots broke out.

Raden Samijaya, too, begged the king to allow Prince Jamojaya to return. He refused to replace his brother as prince. Not only did he love his brother very much, but he himself was only ten years old.

One day, Raden Samijaya disappeared from the palace. He had decided to look for Prince Jamojaya alone. The king ordered all his men to find Raden Samijaya. But, although they searched all over the forest, no one discovered him.

Meanwhile, Raden Samijaya was unable to find Prince Jamojaya. He missed his brother very much. He prayed to the gods and asked them to change his body into that of a bird. He thought that if he became a bird, it would be very easy for him to fly over the forests, mountains, rivers and valleys to find his beloved brother.

The gods heard Raden Samijaya's prayer, and they turned him into a beautiful bird.

Raden Samijaya flew from forest to forest, mountain to mountain and river to river, searching for Prince Jamojaya. One day he arrived at the place where Prince Jamojaya and Dewi Kusumasari had died. After drinking from the spring, he perched on a branch of the banyan tree.

"Brother, brother, brother . . ." he called in sorrow.

No sooner had he finished his call than the leaves of the banyan tree could be heard in answer: "I am your brother. I am your brother. I am your brother."

This was followed by a gentle cry from the spring: "You are sitting on your brother's lap. You are sitting on your brother's lap."

Sadly, the bird could not understand these words. He kept flying, searching everywhere, calling, "Brother, brother, brother . . ."

And although the banyan tree could be heard to answer, "I am your brother. I am your brother. I am your brother," the bird could not understand.

And for all we know, he is still mournfully flying about to this day, seeking the brother he lost.

Masarasenani and the Sun

Once upon a time, there lived a man named Masarasenani. He had a wife and two daughters. The eldest daughter's name was Serawiri, and the youngest was named Serimini.

Every day, the family went to pound at the sago tree to make flour. But the yield was barely enough to keep them alive. At that time, the day was very short. Night came before people could finish pounding the sago. Many of the villagers were starving.

Things continued like this for many, many years.

No one seemed to know what to do, until one day Masarasenani had an idea. He decided to meet with the sun, Masarasitumi.

By chance, Masarasenani knew the place

where Masarasitumi rose. That very morning, he had seen the sun pass by a narrow rift between two hills.

That night, Masarasenani went in secret to that place. Soon he installed a trap to catch the sun.

After he had finished setting the trap, Masarasenani went home. His wife and daughters didn't know about his plan.

The following day, as usual, Masarasenani and his wife and daughters went to pound the sago trees. They worked hard to get as much flour as they could before the sun set.

But what had happened?

Their sago basket was full, and still the night hadn't come. The villagers were astonished! Why hadn't the sun set? The day had been unusually long.

No one knew what was going on except for Masarasenani.

Although Masarasenani was delighted because the villagers could gather more food, he felt restless. He knew that Masarasitumi had been trapped, and that he must be released to do his job and set, so that night could come.

Masarasenani sent his wife and daughters home with the sago they had pounded. He intended to release the sun so it would be dark soon. He hurried to the place where Masarasitumi had been trapped.

Masarasenani's heart was pounding. Through the trees he spied the trap with Masarasitumi in it. He heard the sun lament, "Please, Masarasenani, come quickly. Bring me some gatal leaves to cure my leg that is hurt and swollen because of your trap." Gatal means itch, and its leaves have always been used to cure itching or swelling in that part of Indonesia.

Masarasenani was startled to hear his name. He was surprised that Masarasitumi knew that it was he who had set the trap. The sun's lament touched his heart. He soon appeared from his hiding place to free Masarasitumi.

Seeing Masarasenani coming to help him, the sun said, "Be careful. Approach me only from the back. Otherwise you will be burnt by the rays that pour forth from my face, just like these trees around me."

Masarasenani saw that the trees around the sun were all brown and dried up.

After the sun had been released, he told Masarasenani where he could find gatal leaves to cure his swollen leg, and he told him what the leaves looked like.

Masarasenani gathered as many gatal leaves as he could and carried them back to the place where the sun was waiting. Masarasenani then helped to rub the leaves onto the sun's swollen leg, and not long after that, the sun's leg was cured.

"Masarasenani, why did you want to trap me? What have I done wrong?" asked the sun.

"I am sorry, but my family and all the other villagers were starving. You set before we could gather and pound enough sago and other food, so that the day became dark. We couldn't get enough to eat."

After listening to Masarasenani's complaints, the sun promised to change his behavior. He would try to be fair in dividing the time so that the people could gather enough food.

After Masarasitumi's leg was completely healed, he went back to the western horizon, and Masarasenani went home. He then told his wife and daughters what had happened.

Since then, the sun divides the time equally between day and night. He stays in the sky longer than he did before. The villagers were very happy, because now they could gather enough food.

People call the place where the sun was trapped Mayawer, which means "the trapped sun." The place where Masarasenani picked the gatal leaves is now a forest of gatal bushes. It is said that the gatal leaves of today are not as big as they once were. But the people still use the leaves to cure itching and swelling.

The Tiny Boy

Once upon a time, in a small village at the edge of a forest, there lived a poor farmer with seven children. They lived under desperate conditions. They had a small farm to cultivate and two buffaloes. To support the family, the children would go into the forest to pick up firewood to sell and find fruit to eat.

One day a bad thing happened. A flood washed away everything in the village, including their house and the buffaloes. Their rice paddy that was ready to harvest was also flooded.

After the water subsided, this poor family used the remaining pieces of their house to build a shelter. They lived in abject poverty.

In desperation, the husband approached his wife and said, "Dear, our life is getting harder and harder. I'm afraid we won't be able to feed the children. I'm thinking of abandoning our four bigger sons to reduce our burden. We must let them live on their own. May God bless them all."

At first his wife refused the idea, but she didn't have any alternative. Sadly, she finally agreed with her husband's suggestion.

The following morning, the farmer woke his four older children. He took them to the forest to pick fruit. He led his children far away into the middle of the forest.

The children followed their father eagerly, until finally they arrived in an area they had never seen before. They happily picked as many fruits and plants as they could carry.

Then they rested while they ate the lunch they had brought from home.

"Rest and enjoy your meal," the farmer said to his children. "Let me get you some water from the nearby spring. I'll be back soon."

The children waited and waited, but their father did not come back.

Finally, it grew dark, and they realized that their father had deceived them and had planned to leave them. They began to feel worried and scared.

The oldest child was called Si Kecil, the Tiny Boy. His body was very small, but he was brave and smart. He led his younger brothers to look for shelter. Very late in the afternoon, they found a cave.

While his three brothers were resting in the cave, the Tiny Boy climbed a big tree. From the tree he saw a light in the distance. He led his three brothers there, and the next morning they arrived at a hut.

Finding nobody around, the Tiny Boy peered through a hole in the wall. Inside the hut he saw a giant sleeping. That reminded him of a story he had heard from the villagers, that in the forest there was a fierce giant named Nenekpakande, a man-eater.

"We'd better hide," the Tiny Boy said to his brothers. "The giant will come after us if he sees us. I see so many human bones inside."

When the sun rose, they saw the giant come out of the hut with a machete in hand. Then they hurried into the hut to find something to eat.

After they had eaten, the Tiny Boy said to his brothers, "We must deceive the giant if we want to survive. Get a large rake, three meters of palm fiber and three tortoises. Get them soon!"

After his brothers had collected all this, the Tiny Boy said, "Go up to the top of the hut with these things, and let me wait for Nenekpakande here. If I ask you to drop these things, do it."

The three younger brothers followed his instructions.

Late in the afternoon, they heard the giant's steps from afar — *gedebam-gedebum.*

When the giant arrived in front of the hut, the Tiny Boy stopped him.

"Nenekpakande, do not enter the house," he said.

"Who are you? How dare you stop me?" the giant said furiously. "Don't you know I hunt all kinds of animals and human beings here?"

The Tiny Boy was not afraid. He stood up bravely right in front of the entrance and said, "I know who you are. The villagers often talked about you. I want to let you know that I just saw a bigger, fiercer giant on your roof. He would like to kill you. If you don't believe me, let me call him."

Then the Tiny Boy shouted, "Hey, giant who is staying on the top of the house! Show us your things to convince us how big you are!"

The first thing that fell down to the ground was a huge rake that was shaped like a comb. Nenekpakande thought that it belonged to a real giant who was on top of the house.

Although he was a little bit afraid, Nenekpakande didn't believe the Tiny Boy. "Maybe the boy is right," he thought, "but I want more evidence."

Then he said, "Boy, if it is just a comb, I have an even bigger comb myself."

Hearing this, the Tiny Boy gave another instruction to his brothers. "Hey, giant on the top of the house, show us your hair!"

A huge palm fiber suddenly dropped to the ground.

As it was already dark, Nenekpakande thought the big, long hair was real. He started to feel scared, but he did not want to give up.

"How can I believe you?" he said. "Who knows, this giant may be smaller than I am."

The Tiny Boy shouted once again. "Hey, big giant up there. Throw down three lice from your hair!" Soon three tortoises dropped down and began to creep over Nenekpakande.

In the dark, Nenekpakande could not see what kind of animals were crawling over him. He thought they were lice. Without delay he ran away, helter-skelter, until he finally fell over a cliff to his death.

The Tiny Boy's brothers hurriedly climbed down from the roof, and the four boys began to search the hut.

In one corner there was a huge box tied up with a rope. They opened it with difficulty. Inside the box they saw gold, silver and beautiful diamonds.

They packed everything up and left the giant's hut, taking all the treasure with them. And though it took them some time to find their way, they finally arrived home.

Their parents were surprised to see that their four children had managed to come back, but they were very happy. They actually loved their children very much.

With the wealth the Tiny Boy and his brothers had brought home, they never lacked for food again, and they lived happily ever after.

Ampak and the Cunning Civet Cat

Do you want to know how Ampak became a king? This is the story.

A long, long time ago in a village, there lived a young man named Ampak. All the villagers grew rice except for Ampak. He planted citrus trees.

Ampak loved his citrus trees very much. He tended them all day long. He even slept under the trees.

With such good care, Ampak's citrus trees finally bore fruit. He was so fond of the trees that he counted the fruits every day. One after the other, the villagers came to see his trees, and they were all amazed. That is why they gave him his nickname, "Ampak, King of the Citrus Trees."

One night, Ampak was sound asleep, exhausted after long days of guarding his citrus trees. The night was dark. A cunning musang, a civet cat that had long been spying on the trees, quietly approached Ampak, who was sleeping soundly. The cat climbed up the tree by way of Ampak's shoulder. Ampak didn't wake up, and the cat succeeded in picking a citrus fruit.

The following day, Ampak was very surprised to see that one of his fruits was missing. He was very sad.

"Tonight," he said to himself, "I will spy to see who dares to steal my citrus fruits."

That night, Ampak pretended to fall asleep. Soon the civet cat came stalking and climbed Ampak's shoulder to steal fruit.

The cat had just put one of his legs on his shoulder when Ampak opened his eyes.

"Here you are, you thief," said Ampak angrily. "How dare you steal my fruit? I am going to kill you."

"No!" cried the cat. "Don't kill me, please! If you fulfill my request, you will become a king."

"Are you kidding?" asked Ampak.

"No, believe me," replied Musang. "But first you must give me three more citrus fruits."

"Honest?" asked Ampak, but he gave Musang the fruit.

"Please believe me," said Musang, and Ampak did.

The following day, Musang made a journey. After walking for some time, he arrived at the palace of a very rich king. The courtyard was covered with diamonds and the palace stairs were made of gold.

But the cat did not stop. Instead he continued his journey until he came to another kingdom. This kingdom was very plain and ruled by a single princess.

Musang met the princess and said, "Your Highness, would you like to get married? I am the servant of a very handsome and rich king named Ampak. His palace courtyards are covered with diamonds. The stairs are made of gold. And in the palace there are many luxurious things."

"Are you telling the truth?" asked the princess.

"Yes, Your Highness."

"In that case, I want to meet your king first."

"Well, then, Your Highness, allow me to go home to inform him," replied Musang.

Musang hurried back to the home of Ampak, the King of Citrus.

"Ampak, would you like to get married?" Musang asked.

"Who doesn't want to get married?" replied Ampak.

"Okay, then, you just wait here. And I will inform the princess."

Musang ran back to the princess, who was already assembling her servants and guards to escort her to Ampak's palace.

"What a coincidence," thought the cunning civet cat.

"Let me depart first, Your Highness," Musang said. "And you can catch up later."

After walking for some time, Musang met a herdsman who was tending his cows. He had a lot of cows.

"Hey, herdsman, watch out," Musang warned him. "There are robbers down there. Be careful!"

The herdsman was frightened. "How can I escape the robbers?" he asked.

"Listen! If the leader asks whose cows you are tending, just say that they belong to Ampak," replied the cat.

When the princess met the herdsman, she asked, "Whose cows are all these?"

"They belong to Ampak," said the herdsman.

"Musang was right," thought the princess.

Meanwhile, Musang continued on his journey, and after a while he met a shepherd.

"Hey, shepherd, watch your step. A gang of robbers is coming," said Musang.

"Please help me," said the shepherd, shivering.

"Okay," replied Musang. "The trick is this. If the robbers come, just let them know that all the goats belong to King Ampak. They won't disturb you then."

So when the princess's party arrived, the shepherd explained that all the goats he was herding belonged to King Ampak.

"Wow, how rich he is," said the princess.

After a long journey, the princess arrived at the palace of the rich king, where Musang was waiting.

"Your Highness, please rest with your party here," he said to the princess. "I will go into the palace to meet the king and prepare a welcome ceremony."

Musang then went into the palace and met the king who was in the inner room.

"Your Majesty, I am here to inform you that a gang of robbers has attacked the kingdom. They have many troops, and your soldiers have been defeated," said Musang.

The king was surprised and frightened. "What should I do? I cannot defend myself," he said.

"Leave the matter to me, Your Majesty," Musang replied quickly. "Just go and hide yourself in the attic."

The rich king hastily climbed up to the attic. But in his panic, he slipped and fell into the burning hearth, where he died instantly.

When the princess and her party finally entered the palace, they were amazed. Everything was made of gold and glittering jewels.

After waiting for a long time without any welcome from King Ampak, the princess asked, "Musang, where is your king?"

"Be patient, Your Highness," replied the cunning civet cat. "Our king is hunting. Allow me to bring him here."

Musang ran to search for Ampak. He found him leaning against a beloved citrus tree.

"Ampak, are you ready for a wedding today?" asked Musang.

"I am," replied Ampak. "But my present existence is not like that of a king."

"Don't worry," said Musang. "Go into the river. When the princess comes, just say that you have fallen into the water. In addition, say that you have thrown all your clothes into the river."

When Musang didn't show up, the princess and her party went to catch up with him.

"Hey, Musang, where is your king?" asked the princess.

"He is in the water, Your Highness," answered Musang, pointing to Ampak.

"How strange! Why would a king stay submerged in the water?"

"I slipped and fell into the river," replied Ampak. "It was a very hot day. I wanted to take a bath and I took off my clothes. It seems that my

clothes have washed away. So I must stay submerged and wait for my guards to pass by."

"Well, then, let's return to the palace and get married," said the princess.

Later Ampak came out of the river and put on royal clothes that Musang brought him. They all went merrily back to the palace.

The wedding ceremony of Ampak and the princess was very grand. The people from the two kingdoms were happy and gay. Many entertainments were held. And from that moment, Ampak really became a king.

After that day, Ampak no longer took care of his beloved citrus trees. He became a just and wise king, ruling his kingdom together with the queen.

As for Musang the cunning civet cat, he refused to live in the palace. Instead, he replaced Ampak and guarded his citrus trees.

Senggutru

Once upon a time in a small village, there was chaos. An evil giant came to the village to look for food. Parents panicked and hurriedly took their children to other villages. They were afraid that their children would be eaten by the furious giant.

In the village there lived a poor widow with her daughter, who was named Senggutru. Senggutru was the only child who was not taken away by her mother, for they had no relatives who could help take care of her. Besides, Senggutru's mother was sure that Senggutru could take care of herself. She was very small, as small as a thumb. Whenever the giant came, she could hide herself somewhere under the equipment or utensils inside the house.

Every time the giant came to the village, Senggutru would look for a hiding place. She knew that the giant was coming long before he entered her house. His steps and the sound of crashing cooking utensils indicated that he was starving and looking for food.

The giant could never catch Senggutru, for she was always moving. She would hide in the kukusan rice steamer, under the tudung saji that was used to cover the food, or in the rice basket, the frying pan or the cooking pot.

Because the giant often came to the house, Senggutru dared to make fun of him.

"Uncle Giant, Uncle Giant," she would call. "You are a stupid giant. My fat is delicious, far more delicious than the porridge you just ate."

Since Senggutru was very small, the giant could barely hear her, and he couldn't tell where her voice was coming from. So every time he came to Senggutru's house, he had to be satisfied with only a very small bowl of porridge before he continued his hunt for other victims. The porridge was actually Senggutru's lunch, so the giant was, of course, still starving.

One day, as usual, before Senggutru's mother went to the market, she prepared a bowl of porridge for Senggutru.

"Be careful, darling!" she said to her daughter.

"Take good care of yourself. Go and hide quickly as soon as you hear the giant coming."

"Yes, Mother," said Senggutru as her mother left the house. Because she was so tiny, it was impossible for her to help her mother in the market.

Instead, Senggutru cut a palm leaf rib, or lidi, into thin slivers with a little knife. People in the village often made pincuk, a kind of food container made from a banana leaf. The square-shaped leaf could be folded and fastened with a piece of lidi to form a container.

A few moments later, Senggutru heard heavy steps. She hurried to hide under a tudung saji. She still held the little knife tightly.

When the giant arrived at Senggutru's house, he began to search for something to eat. He ate up Senggutru's tiny bowl of porridge. But then he did not leave the house as usual. He rested for a moment, right beside the tudung saji.

Suddenly, the giant sneezed. The tudung saji where Senggutru was hiding blew away. Senggutru tried to run, but it was too late, and the giant saw her.

He picked up Senggutru with his two big fingers and lifted her high.

"Ha, ha, ha. Finally I have caught you, Senggutru," he cried happily. "Too bad I have eaten your porridge. It would be more delicious to eat porridge with small girl meat."

The giant was about to swallow Senggutru. He opened his mouth wide, and she saw his big sharp teeth.

Suddenly a thought struck her.

"I will be pulverized if the giant chews me up. I'd better jump into his stomach." So no sooner had the giant loosened his squeeze, than Senggutru jumped into his stomach.

It was very dark inside the giant's stomach. Senggutru tried to feel where she was. She groped around with her knife.

"Senggutru, do not stab my intestine!" the giant cried painfully. When he cried, he opened his mouth wide so that light shone into his insides. Senggutru could see his long white intestine.

Now she had an idea.

"If I stab his stomach, the giant will cry. And there will be light so that I can find my way out."

Meanwhile, inside the giant's stomach, Senggutru began to grow bigger.

While she groped and climbed out of his stomach, her knife accidentally jabbed into the giant's liver.

"Senggutru, do not stab my liver!" shouted the giant in pain.

"Spit me out," answered Senggutru.

"No way," cried the giant. When he shouted, his mouth opened wide again, and light came in.

Senggutru jumped higher, reaching the gi-

ant's heart. He shouted in pain when she took hold of his heart. His cry was so loud that she was thrown out of his mouth.

Senggutru ran away as fast as she could. The giant tried to catch her, but after a few steps he fell onto the ground and died.

Senggutru slowly approached the giant's body. He really was big and terrifying.

When Senggutru's mother arrived home from the market, she looked at Senggutru in great wonder. Her daughter's body was no longer small. Senggutru had grown into a normal girl, and she even looked pretty. Senggutru later told her mother what had happened and took her to the back yard to see the dead giant.

Soon the news spread all over the village. The villagers came in throngs to see the giant. They thanked God that they could live peacefully again, and their children no longer needed to flee.

And Senggutru, the brave girl, became the heroine and pride of the village.

Princess Kemang

There was once a kingdom that lay on the outskirts of a dense forest. The king had a daughter who was fond of hunting, fishing and hiking in the woods. Princess Kemang had even been called up to serve as a soldier in the army. She had mastered sword fighting. She was excellent with the bow and arrow, and she handled a spear as well as any man.

One day the princess went hunting for deer. She carried her sword and her bow. Her beloved dog went with her. The princess walked from one forest to another, from one meadow to another, and from one hill to another. She rafted across many rivers, and swam across others.

Eventually, after a long journey, Princess Kemang spotted a striped-leg deer. She shot her arrow quickly, but missed. Angry at this, she chased after the deer. Wherever it ran, she was right behind. Not for a second did she take her eyes off the animal.

The deer ran deep into the woods. Then suddenly it stopped under a kemang tree.

As Princess Kemang came near, she realized that the tree was calling to her.

"Dear Princess, don't chase after this deer. It is actually a tiger in disguise."

Princess Kemang was startled to hear the tree give her this advice. But she was determined to kill the deer. So she climbed the tree and shot her arrow straight through the deer's body.

The instant it died, the deer indeed transformed into a tiger.

The princess leapt down from the tree to skin it, and something even stranger happened. The kemang tree moved and slowly turned into a handsome young man.

"Who are you? How can you change your form like this?" exclaimed the princess.

"I am the guardian of this forest," he answered.

"Come with me and we will hunt together," she pleaded.

"I can't leave until everything in the forest has changed to its human form and the forest has turned into a kingdom."

"All right," replied the princess. "I promise that if the forest becomes a kingdom, I will return for you. I want to be your friend."

After uttering these words, the princess continued her hunt, leaving the handsome man standing guard in the forest.

Some time later, Princess Kemang met a cat. The princess's dog barked fiercely. But instead of running away, the cat began to grow. The dog barked more ferociously, but the cat grew even bigger. And then suddenly, it pounced on the dog and swallowed it!

Princess Kemang was distraught at the loss of her dear dog. She sadly turned to go back home. She walked alone now.

When she came to the river, it was infested with crocodiles, and she could not cross. The crocs looked very hungry.

"Princess, now your life comes to an end," said the biggest crocodile. "You will be our meal."

"Crocodile," the princess replied, "I understand that you are big and strong. But I can fight a thousand crocodiles."

"Really? I want to see this. Let me call my friends. We will see then if you can fight one thousand of us!"

"All right. Line up so I can count you. I want to make sure there are really one thousand of you before the battle begins."

So the crocodiles came and formed a line. There were so many that they stretched from one side of the river to the other.

The princess quickly jumped onto the back of the first crocodile.

"This is one," she called. "This is two." She jumped onto the back of the second crocodile. "Three . . . four . . . five . . ." And, jumping from back to back as she counted, she easily crossed the wide river.

She jumped ashore and called out loudly, "Thank you, crocodiles! You are too greedy. How could you feed yourselves with just my small meat anyway? Look for another meal. There are a lot of rivers on the earth."

How angry the crocodiles were. They realized how stupid they had been.

When Princess Kemang arrived at the palace, she told the king and queen all about her journey.

A year later, the princess was out hunting again. She found herself in a huge wood and walked along a long river there. After three days she came upon a large kingdom. She was very surprised to see a kingdom right in the forest.

She met an old man.

"What is the name of this kingdom?" she asked. "And who is the ruler here?"

"This is Kemang Kingdom. Prince Kemang

is the king. Once this was a dense forest. It was called Ghost Forest, because the entire forest was occupied by spirits. Prince Kemang was a god who had been cursed by the gods in heaven. He became a large kemang tree that grew in the middle of the forest. The gods' curse said that if a human spoke to the tree, it would change into a human again, and the forest could become a kingdom."

Princess Kemang remembered her past journey through this forest.

"Old man, please take me to Prince Kemang," she said. And, accompanied by the old man, Princess Kemang went to the palace.

When they met, the prince said, "Dear Princess, you are the hunter who met me last year, aren't you?"

"Yes, it is I," answered the princess. "I come to fulfill my promise."

They promised to become friends, and Princess Kemang invited Prince Kemang to visit her kingdom. So they traveled together. Their journey took five days.

The king approached them with happiness. He welcomed the prince with food and drink and asked where he had come from. The king was very surprised to hear the prince's story. He asked him to become his son-in-law. So the servants were commanded to prepare a royal wedding party. It was celebrated for seven days and seven nights.

When the king became old, he gave his throne to his daughter. The two kingdoms were united into a large and victorious kingdom. And they lived happily ever after.

ABOUT THE STORIES

PRINCESS MANDALIKA

A popular folktale among the Sasak ethnic group living on Lombok Island in the province of West Nusa Tenggara. I was first told this story by a taxi driver when I visited Lombok in 2000. Every year in February and March, the people in Lombok celebrate the tradition of Bau Nyale, when they catch sea creatures believed to be the incarnation of Princess Mandalika. This feast is considered to be a blessing, as this worm-like creature is extremely nutritious, with a very high protein content.

This story also appears in my book, *Putri Mandalika / Princess Mandalika* (Jakarta: Kelompok Pencinta Bacaan Anak, 2005).

In the Stith Thompson motif index, the story is listed under A2182 Origin of worm.

HUA LO PUU

A rare folktale from North Maluku, told originally in the Ternate language. My source is *Folktales from Maluku Province*, Department of Education and Culture, Inventory and Documentation of Regional Culture Project (Jakarta, 1982).

Stories of ungrateful children are found in all cultures in Indonesia. It is rare to find a story that teaches parents not to neglect their children. This story has also been published in my retelling, *Hua Lo Puu / Hua Lo Poo* (Jakarta: Kelompok Pencinta Bacaan Anak, 2005). It is popular with both children and their parents.

In the Stith Thompson motif index, the story is found under R131ff Exposed or abandoned child rescued; and D150 Transformation: man to bird.

THE LEGEND OF THE BANYAN TREE

On the Indonesian islands that have Hindu influences, such as Java, Madura and Bali, the banyan tree is considered sacred, and it is looked upon as the abode of both good and bad spirits. This little-known Javanese story is my retelling and interpretation, taken from *De legende van den Waringin Boom, Javaansche Sagen, Mythen en Legenden — versameld door* [collected by] Jos Meyboom, second edition (Zutphen: W.J. Thieme & Cie, 1928). It is also found in my book, *Legenda Pohon Beringin / The Legend of the Banyan Tree* (Jakarta: Kelompok Pencinta Bacaan Anak, 2001), and in *Indonesian Folktales* (Westport, Connecticut: Libraries Unlimited, 2003).

In the Stith Thompson motif index, the story is under the number A2681.10 Origin of banyan tree.

MASARASENANI AND THE SUN

This story was originally told in the Windesi indigenous language. The source is *Folktales from West Irian Jaya* (now Papua), Department of Education and Culture, Inventory and Documentation of Regional Culture Project (Jakarta, 1983). The story is also found in my book, *Masarasenani dan Matahari / Masarasenani and the Sun* (Jakarta: Kelompok Pencinta Bacaan Anak, 2006).

In the Stith Thompson motif index, the story is under A1017.1 Man's desire for sun; and H1317.1.1 Quest for place where sun rises.

THE TINY BOY

This story originated in South Sulawesi Province and was originally told in the Bugis indigenous language. Stories of small heroes are also found in "Senggutru," a Javanese folktale about a thumbling, and in "Princess Jasmine," a folktale from North Sumatera about a princess whose body is as small as a jasmine blossom.

The source for this story is *Folktales from South Sulawesi*

Province, Department of Education and Culture, Inventory and Documentation of Regional Culture Project (Jakarta, 1984). I have also retold this story in *Si Kecil / Tiny Boy* (Jakarta: Kelompok Pencinta Bacaan Anak, 2001).

In the Stith Thompson motif index, this story is under L311 Weak (small) hero overcomes large fighter; and G520 Ogre deceived into self-injury.

AMPAK AND THE CUNNING CIVET CAT

This story originated in South Kalimantan Province and was told in the Banjar indigenous language. The source is *Folktales from South Kalimantan Province*, Department of Education and Culture, Inventory and Documentation of Regional Culture Project (Jakarta, 1984). In my retelling, Ampak and the civet cat are equally important, since it is due to the cleverness of the cat that Ampak gains his fortune and becomes a king. This story is also found in my picture book, *Ampak dan Musang yang Cerdik / Ampak and the Cunning Civet Cat* (Jakarta: Kelompok Pencinta Bacaan Anak, 2008).

In the Stith Thompson motif index, this story appears under B582.1.1 Animal wins wife for his master; K1917.3 Penniless wooer: Helpful animal reports master wealthy and thus wins girl for him; and K1952.1.1 Poor boy said by helpful animal to be dispossessed prince who has lost clothes while swimming.

SENGGUTRU

This folktale comes from Central Java Province on Java Island. My retelling in *Senggutru* (Jakarta: Kelompok Pencinta Bacaan Anak, 2001) stops when the heroine defeats the giant, since this is the version I first heard when I was a child. Another version written by Dr. G.A.J. Hazeu (Batawi: Kantoor Tjitak, Ruygrok & Co, 1911) continues the story. One day Senggutru is taken by a spirit and put in a tree, and she can't climb down until a prince rescues her and marries her. This typical happy ending from the old times shows that a girl can raise her status by marrying a prince. The story of the innocent girl who is pitted against a giant is also found in stories like *Timun Mas (Golden Cucumber)* from Java and *Siti Minamina Anak Angkat Sang Raksasa (Siti Minamina the Giant's Adopted Child)* from Maluku.

In the Stith Thompson motif index, this story is listed under L311 Weak (small) hero overcomes larger fighter; L311.4 Little innocent girl is able to drive giant out of land; G512.1 Ogre killed with knife (sword); and F.535.1 Thumbling, person the size of a thumb.

PRINCESS KEMANG

This is a folktale from Bengkulu Province on Sumatera Island, originally told in the Serawai language. This story is also found in my book, *Putri Kemang/Princess Kemang* (Jakarta: Kelompok Pencinta Bacaan Anak, 2005), and in *Indonesian Folktales* (Westport, Connecticut: Libraries Unlimited, 2003). The source is *Folktales from Bengkulu Province*, Department of Education and Culture, Inventory and Documentation of Regional Culture Project (Jakarta, 1982).

In the Stith Thompson motif index, this story is found under F565 Women warriors or hunters; N773 Adventures from pursuing enchanted animal (hind, boar, bird); D659.10 Transformation to lure hunters to a certain place; D431.2 Transformation: tree to person; D215.8 Transformation: man (woman) to mango tree; and K579.2 Monkey in danger on bridge of crocodiles pretends that king has ordered them counted.

GLOSSARY

beringin – banyan tree

gatal – itch

kecil – small

kendi – clay pot

kukusan – rice steamer

lidi – palm leaf rib

musang – a civet cat, a small nocturnal mammal found in Southeast Asia

nyale – a type of sea worm

patih – chief royal assistant who relays the wishes of the ruler

pincuk – a food container made from a banana leaf

sago – a kind of tree and the edible starch that is made from its trunk

tudung saji – a food covering, often made from woven palm strands